My Weird School Graphic Novel: Mr. Corbett Is in Orbit!

Text copyright © 2021 by Dan Gutman

Illustrations copyright © 2021 by Jim Paillot

All rights reserved. Printed in Spain.

www.harpercollinschildrens.com

ISBN 978-0-06-294761-1 (pbk. bdg.) — ISBN 978-0-06-294762-8 (hardcover bdg.)

Typography by Martha Maynard

20 21 22 23 24   EP   10 9 8 7 6 5 4 3 2 1

❖

First Edition

Warning!

THIS BOOK CONTAINS SCENES OF GRAPHIC VIOLINS. READING IT MAY CAUSE SIDE EFFECTS SUCH AS DIZZINESS, RUNNY NOSE, HEARTBURN, SWELLING, AND ITCHY LIPS. READ ONLY AS DIRECTED. KEEP OUT OF REACH OF CHILDREN. AVOID CONTACT WITH EYES. IF SWALLOWED, GET MEDICAL HELP RIGHT AWAY. IF RASH DEVELOPS, DISCONTINUE USE. STORE AT ROOM TEMPERATURE.

YOU CAN'T SAY WE DIDN'T WARN YOU. WELL, YOU CAN SAY IT, BUT YOU'LL BE LYING. IF YOU WANT TO READ A HEARTWARMING GRAPHIC NOVEL ABOUT CUTE PUPPIES, YOU PICKED THE WRONG BOOK.

To all the kids who have read **My Weird School**, and all the parents, teachers, and librarians who have shared the books with their sons, daughters, and students

Table of Contents*

*I DON'T SEE ANY **TABLE**. WHAT DO **TABLES** HAVE TO DO WITH ANYTHING?

CHAPTER 1

The Beginning

READER SURVEY

THIS IS OUR FIRST MY WEIRD SCHOOL GRAPHIC NOVEL. PLEASE TAKE THIS SHORT SURVEY TO HELP US KNOW WHAT YOU LIKE OR DON'T LIKE . . .

WHAT DO YOU THINK OF THE BOOK SO FAR?
- I LIKE IT
- I DON'T LIKE IT
- NONE OF YOUR BEESWAX
- I LIKE HOT DOGS
- WHAT DO HOT DOGS HAVE TO DO WITH ANYTHING?

DID THIS BOOK MAKE YOU . . .
- LAUGH
- CRY
- WANT TO READ ANOTHER MY WEIRD SCHOOL BOOK
- VOMIT

IF YOU WERE STRANDED ON A DESERT ISLAND AND THIS BOOK WAS WATERPROOF, WOULD YOU USE IT TO BUILD A LIFE RAFT?

WOULD YOU RECOMMEND THIS BOOK TO A DOG?
- YES
- NO
- YES AND NO
- IT DEPENDS ON THE DOG

HOW ABOUT TO A HAMSTER?

WHERE DID YOU GET THIS BOOK?
- AT A BOOKSTORE
- AT A LIBRARY
- ONLINE
- FROM A FRIEND
- FROM A GUY ON THE CORNER WEARING A TRENCH COAT

DID YOU TAKE A SHOWER OR BATH THIS WEEK? IF SO, PLEASE GIVE IT BACK.

WHAT DO YOU CALL A GUY HANGING ON A WALL?
- BOB
- WALLY
- ART
- DUMBHEAD

WHY DO BAGPIPERS WALK WHILE THEY PLAY?
- TO GET TO THE OTHER SIDE
- THEY'RE TRYING TO FIND A BATHROOM
- SO PEOPLE DON'T THROW ROTTEN FRUIT AT THEM
- THEY'RE TRYING TO GET AWAY FROM THE MUSIC

WHEN YOU FINISH READING THIS BOOK, YOU WILL . . .
- READ IT AGAIN
- DONATE IT TO A LIBRARY
- LEND IT TO A FRIEND
- USE IT TO GET YOUR CAMPFIRE STARTED
- EAT IT

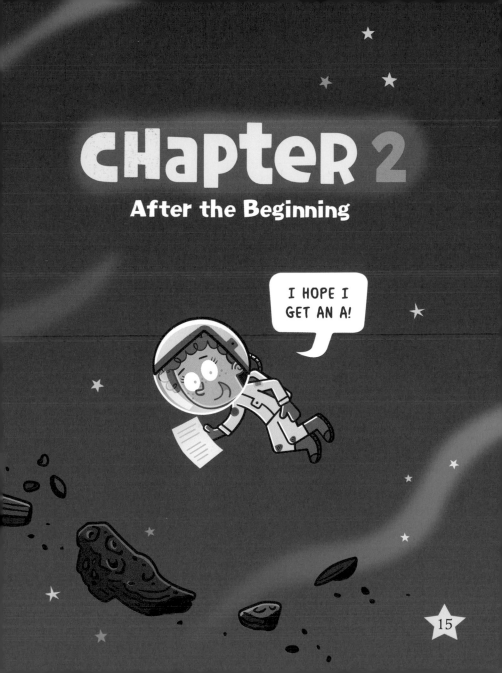

WILL MR. COOPER'S CLASS PLEASE REPORT TO THE ALL-PURPOSE ROOM?

NOT AGAIN!

THE ALL-PORPOISE ROOM

PRINGLE UP, EVERYBODY!

CAN I BE THE LINE LEADER?

CAN I BE THE DOOR HOLDER?

NASA IS THE COOLEST PLACE
IN THE HISTORY OF THE WORLD!

23

That's when the weirdest thing in the history of the world happened!

CHAPTER 3

Almost the Middle

Everybody was yelling and screaming and hooting and hollering and freaking out!

THE FIRST RULE OF BEING A KID

BREAKING NEWS

WASHINGTON, 11:27 A.M. EST

NEWS NEWS NEWS NEWS NEWS NEWS NEWS NEWS NEWS NEWS NO NEWS IS GOOD NEWS . . . NEW
NEWS FOR YOU . . . WE HAVE A NOSE FOR NEWS . . . NEWS THAT JUST HAPPENED . . . NEWS NEW
HAPPENING NOW . . . NEWS THAT WILL HAPPEN LATER . . . NEWS THAT WILL NEVER HAPPEN .
SURE ARE . . . HAPPENING RIGHT NOW . . .

THIS IS TAB BATTAN WITH BREAKING NEWS. THE LARGEST ROCKET IN THE WORLD, NASA'S SPACE LAUNCH SYSTEM, HAS BEEN ACCIDENTALLY LAUNCHED AND IS NOW HURTLING INTO OUTER SPACE. WE'LL BRING YOU MORE INFORMATION ABOUT THIS STORY AS IT DEVELOPS. BUT THE TOP STORY OF THE DAY CONCERNS THE JARDISHIAN FAMILY . . .

TOP STORY
news you need more than food and air.

LIVE
BNN

'S NEWS. . . WE HAVE GOOD NEWS AND BAD
'S NEWS NEWS NEWS . . . NEWS THAT IS
NEWS . . . ARE YOU SICK OF NEWS YET? WE

CHAPTER 5

After the Middle

51

I WONDER IF THE HUBBLE SPACE TELESCOPE WAS NAMED AFTER MAYOR HUBBLE.

CHapteR 6

More Stuff Happens Here

It was so quiet, you could hear a pin drop. But why would anybody bring a pin into outer space? That would be dumb. Somebody might get hurt! But it was really quiet.

60

CHapteR 7

Getting Exciting!

CHAPTeR 8
Almost the End

It was **Mr. Granite,** our old teacher!

73

(*That's grown-up talk for "What are you doing here?")

(*That's a prize they give to people who don't have bells.)

BREAKING NEWS

THIS IS TAB BATTAN WITH BREAKING NEWS. A GIANT BEACH UMBRELLA HAS BEEN SPOTTED IN OUTER SPACE BETWEEN THE SUN AND THE EARTH. IT IS BLOCKING A PORTION OF THE SUN'S RAYS AND APPEARS TO BE THE SOLUTION TO THE CLIMATE-CHANGE PROBLEM. AT THIS POINT, WE DO NOT KNOW IF THE UMBRELLA IS CONNECTED IN ANY WAY TO THE NASA ROCKET THAT WAS ACCIDENTALLY LAUNCHED SEVERAL HOURS AGO. IN THE TOP STORY OF THE DAY, WE HAVE OBTAINED A COPY OF THE RECEIPT FROM THE JARDISHIAN FAMILY'S SHOPPING TRIP . . .

WASHINGTON, 2:15 P.M. EST

A CORNUCOPIA OF NEWS . . . BAD STUFF HAPPENING 24/7 . . . COTTON CANDY STOCKS PLUMMET . . . THERE WAS A FIRE SOMEWHERE . . . CELEBRITIES WALKING DOWN THE STREET HOLDING COFFEE CUPS . . . WATCH US OR GET A LIFE . . . SOMEBODY GOT CAUGHT DOING BAD STUFF . . . MEANINGLESS INFO THAT DOESN'T CONCERN YOU . . . WHY ARE YOU STILL READING THIS? IF YOU TURN US OFF, YOU'LL BE SORRY . . .

LIVE

BNN

CHAPTER 9
The End

(*But not with glue, that would be weird.)

A NOTE FOR THE READER

IT'S EXTREMELY DOUBTFUL THAT ANYONE WILL DEPLOY A GIANT BEACH UMBRELLA IN OUTER SPACE, OR THAT THIS WOULD BE A SOLUTION TO CLIMATE CHANGE. IF YOU WANT TO HELP PROTECT THE PLANET, HERE ARE SOME REAL, PRACTICAL THINGS YOU CAN DO . . .

Educate Your Parents!

WHEN YOU WERE YOUNGER, YOUR PARENTS TAUGHT YOU HOW TO RIDE A BIKE, HOW TO TIE YOUR SHOES, AND HOW TO CATCH A BALL. NOW, IT'S UP TO **YOU** TO EDUCATE **THEM**. CONVINCE **THEM** TO VOTE FOR POLITICIANS WHO WILL PROTECT OUR ENVIRONMENT INSTEAD OF DESTROY IT. THIS IS NOT A REPUBLICAN OR DEMOCRATIC ISSUE. DOESN'T **EVERYONE** WANT TO LIVE IN A SAFE, CLEAN WORLD? FIND OUT WHICH CANDIDATES ARE ENDORSED BY ENVIRONMENTAL GROUPS SUCH AS THE SIERRA CLUB AND GREENPEACE. CONVINCE YOUR PARENTS TO SUPPORT THOSE CANDIDATES.

Contact Politicians!

REMIND THEM THAT **YOU** ARE THE FUTURE. TELL THEM HOW IMPORTANT IT IS TO PROTECT OUR PLANET. GET YOUR CLASS TO WRITE LETTERS. YOUR TEACHER CAN HELP YOU FIND THE ADDRESS OF YOUR LOCAL POLITICAL LEADERS.

GET YOUR SCHOOL INVOLVED!

FORM A CLUB OF KIDS WHO CARE ABOUT THE ENVIRONMENT.
START A PETITION. MAKE YOUR VOICE HEARD.

Get Started!
HERE ARE SOME WEBSITES WHERE YOU CAN GET MORE INFORMATION.

CLIMATE KIDS: CLIMATEKIDS.NASA.GOV/CLIMATE-CHANGE-MEANING

NATIONAL GEOGRAPHIC KIDS: WWW.NATGEOKIDS.COM/UK/DISCOVER
/GEOGRAPHY/GENERAL-GEOGRAPHY/WHAT-IS-CLIMATE-CHANGE

GREENPEACE: WWW.GREENPEACE.ORG/USA

SIERRA CLUB: WWW.SIERRACLUB.ORG/HOME

CENTER FOR CLIMATE CHANGE AND ENERGY SOLUTIONS:
WWW.C2ES.ORG/CONTENT/CLIMATE-BASICS-FOR-KIDS

NATURAL RESOURCES DEFENSE COUNCIL: WWW.NRDC.ORG

ENVIRONMENTAL DEFENSE FUND: WWW.EDF.ORG

EARTH DAY NETWORK: WWW.EARTHDAY.ORG